DRA

LIVE
and Let
FLY

adapted by Cordelia Evans

SIMON SPOTLIGHT
New York   London   Toronto   Sydney   New Delhi

SIMON SPOTLIGHT
An imprint of Simon & Schuster Children's Publishing Division
1230 Avenue of the Americas, New York, New York 10020
This Simon Spotlight edition September 2015
DreamWorks Dragons © 2015 DreamWorks Animation LLC. All Rights Reserved.
For information about special discounts for bulk purchases, please contact Simon & Schuster Special Sales
at 1-866-506-1949 or business@simonandschuster.com.
Manufactured in the United States of America 0815 LAK
1 2 3 4 5 6 7 8 9 10
ISBN 978-1-4814-4120-9
ISBN 978-1-4814-4121-6 (eBook)

Fishlegs sat strapped to a chair in a dimly lit cave under Berk.

"Tell us what you know about the dragons, boy," said a voice. "Tell us how you train them."

"I won't talk!" Fishlegs declared. "You can't make me!"

All of a sudden, the few lighted torches in the cave went out, and Fishlegs was plunged into total darkness.

"Okay, okay," he whimpered. "Hiccup is the leader of the Berk Dragon Academy. He rides a Night Fury named Toothless." Fishlegs went on to describe all his friends and their dragons.

When Fishlegs stopped talking, a Night Fury plasma blast lit up the cave, and Fishlegs faced Hiccup, Astrid, Snotlout, Tuffnut, and Ruffnut. They did not look happy.

"What?" asked Fishlegs. "You know I hate the dark!"

Hiccup sighed. "Fishlegs, you can't cave in. Alvin will do a lot more than turn out the light to get you to talk." Hiccup was trying to protect his friends from Alvin the Treacherous, the leader of the Outcast tribe, who wanted to learn the secrets of dragon training—and use them to take over Berk.

So the Dragon Riders were practicing how to keep silent if they were ever captured by Alvin. And Fishlegs had just failed.

The next day Hiccup walked through Berk with his father, Chief Stoick. All around them, the villagers were preparing in case Alvin and his Outcasts attacked.

"From this point forward, there is a ban on flying. Period," Stoick said.

"But that's . . . that's ridiculous," Hiccup stuttered.

"Are you calling your father ridiculous?" asked Stoick.

"Of course not," said Hiccup. "I would never call my father ridiculous. I'm calling my chief ridiculous."

"Dad, Alvin has his own dragons," Hiccup said. "Changewings, Scauldrons, Whispering Deaths. I saw them with my own eyes. If Alvin learns how to train his dragons, and he attacks with them, our only chance is to fight back with ours."

"I understand that. But I'm not going to risk your life or the lives of any of your Dragon Riders. This is my final word," Stoick proclaimed.

When Hiccup broke the news of the ban on flying to the other members of the Dragon Academy, they were furious.

"So what am I supposed to do with Hookfang if he can't fly?" Snotlout whined. "You know what happens when his 'inner warrior' is caged up?" As if on cue, Hookfang's tail burst into flames and he whacked Snotlout with it, sending him flying across the arena.

Hiccup looked at Snotlout. "I'll keep working on my dad," he said.

The sun was going down as Astrid and Hiccup walked home. All of
a sudden Toothless started flapping his wings and running in circles
around Hiccup.

"What's with him?" asked Astrid.

"It's the sunset," Hiccup replied sadly. "We always take a lap around
the island when it gets dark. He loves it."

Hiccup spent his evening in the blacksmith's shop building a wooden shield with a hidden rope. Press a button and the rope would burst out of the shield and tie up an enemy.

"If we can't ride dragons, we have to defend ourselves somehow," he explained.

"You know, Hiccup, your father is just trying to keep you safe," said Gobber.

"I know," Hiccup said. "But the problem is that the safest place for me is on Toothless."

Hiccup wanted to fly as much as Toothless did. So despite Stoick's rule, they were soon up in the air, soaring around Berk.

Hiccup thought they were hidden in the dark, but Astrid had followed them on Stormfly.

"You were just going to fly around at night all by yourself and say nothing?" Astrid asked accusingly.

"I didn't want to get anyone else in trouble," Hiccup protested.

"If you're going to ride dragons behind your father's back, we *all* need to ride dragons behind your father's back," said Astrid.

So they formed a secret Dragon Flight Club and went about recruiting the other Dragon Riders.

"It's a secret dragon flying society," Astrid explained to Snotlout. "We train at night, under the cover of darkness."

Snotlout turned to Hookfang. "What do you think?" Hookfang flamed up immediately, blasting his rider.

"Ahhh!" yelled Snotlout. "He's in."

Next they visited the twins, who had a little trouble understanding the rules of the Dragon Flight Club.

"The first rule of Dragon Flight Club is that there is no Dragon Flight Club," Hiccup said. "Get it?"

"Absolutely not," said Tuffnut.

Luckily, Fishlegs caught on quickly, even if he was hesitant to wake Meatlug from her beauty sleep.

That night after sunset the newly formed Dragon Flight Club met at the Academy.

"We need to be ready for riders on any type of dragon," Hiccup said to the group. "So, I've put together some training exercises—"

"Blah, blah, blah," Snotlout interrupted. "Can we go already?"

They mounted their dragons and set off for the first stop: Changewing Island.

There, the Dragon Riders watched Changewings hunt a pack of wild boars. The chameleon-like dragons changed colors to blend in with the rocks and trees so they could sneak up on their prey.

Hiccup and his friends sat high in the trees, safe from the dragons—until Tuffnut shouted and the Changewings started chasing them!

The Dragon Riders took off and escaped the pursuing dragons by flying high in the sky where the Changewings had nothing to camouflage themselves against.

The next night they were caught in a similar chase, this time pursued by a giant Typhoomerang.

"Hey, Hiccup!" Tuffnut shouted as they raced through clouds. "When did your dad join Dragon Flight Club?"

"He didn't," said Hiccup.

"Weird—'cause he's right there!" Tuffnut pointed. Stoick was below them, riding on his Thunderdrum dragon, Thornado!

"All right, guys, split up, head home, and please keep the dragons out of sight!" Hiccup ordered. They scattered and raced back toward Berk. Everyone got home without being found by Stoick . . . except Fishlegs.

Gobber and Stoick tried to get Fishlegs to tell them about the Dragon Flight Club, but this time Fishlegs wasn't budging.

"My name is Fishlegs. I live on the island of Berk. I don't know anything about dragons or those who ride them." He repeated this over and over until finally Stoick let him go.

The next night, at the Academy, the Dragon Riders were congratulating Fishlegs on staying strong when Snotlout rode in on Hookfang.

"Snotlout, what did I tell you? My dad is on to us. No dragons!" Hiccup said.

"Well, I may have saved this entire island," Snotlout boasted. "Alvin and the Outcasts are attacking as we speak!"

Hiccup ran to wake his father and tell him that the Outcasts were on their way to Berk.

"How would you know that?" asked Stoick. "I told you no flying."

"I've been thinking about that," Hiccup said, looking at his dad accusingly. "Doesn't a ban on dragon flying pertain to all dragons? Even, let's say, a Thunderdrum?"

"We'll talk about this later," Stoick grumbled, not wanting to admit that he had broken his own rule. "Wake the others."

He opened the front door to find Astrid, Snotlout, Ruffnut, Tuffnut, Fishlegs, and their dragons ready to fly.

As they approached Alvin's fleet, Stoick shared his attack plan with Hiccup.

"I'm going to draw their first round of fire," the chief said. "When they're reloading, you attack. But not before."

Sure enough, when Alvin saw Stoick and Thornado above him, he started launching his catapults.

"Now, Hiccup!" Stoick commanded. Hiccup and the other Dragon Riders fired down at Alvin's fleet.

But Alvin had a backup plan. "Open the cargo hold!" he yelled. Several large, angry Changewings flew out from inside the ship and raced into the sky.

"We can't let them get to Berk!" yelled Astrid.

"Astrid, you and the others herd them toward Changewing Island," said Hiccup. "I'm going to help my dad."

"Got it," Astrid said, and she and the rest of the Dragon Riders took off after the Changewings, firing at them to keep them moving.

Hiccup turned back to the Outcasts. Toothless shot a plasma blast at the fleet that hit just as Thornado sent a thunderclap blast. The two blasts combined to create a big explosion.

Thornado and Toothless fired together again.

With their Changewings halfway back to Changewing Island, and the double firepower of Thornado and Toothless, Alvin and the Outcasts had no hope of winning. They soon retreated back to Outcast Island.

Back at their house Stoick apologized to Hiccup.

"I don't like that you disobeyed me, son," he said. "But I can admit when I was wrong. I shouldn't have grounded the dragons. I was just being a father."

"I understand, Dad," Hiccup said.

"Now, tell me about this Dragon Flight Club of yours," Stoick said. "And don't leave out a thing."

"Well," said Hiccup. "The first thing you have to remember is that there is no Dragon Flight Club . . ."